THE KING'S SERVICE

BY

ROBERT E. HOWARD

British Library Cataloguing-in-Publication Data
A catalogue record for this book is available from the
British Library

Contents

Robert E. Howard

Robert Ervin Howard was born in Peaster, Texas in 1906. During his youth, his family moved between a variety of Texan boomtowns, and Howard – a bookish and somewhat introverted child – was steeped in the violent myths and legends of the Old South. Although he loved reading and learning, Howard developed a distinctly Texan, hardboiled outlook on the world. He became a passionate fan of boxing, taking it up at an amateur level, and from the age of nine began to write adventure tales of semi-historical bloodshed. In 1919, when Howard was thirteen, his family moved to the Central Texas hamlet of Cross Plains, where he would stay for the rest of his life.

At fifteen Howard began to read the pulp magazines of the day, and to write more seriously. The December 1922 issue of his high school newspaper featured two of his stories, 'Golden Hope Christmas' and 'West is West'. In 1924 he sold his first piece – a short caveman tale titled 'Spear and Fang' – for $16 to the not-yet-famous *Weird Tales* magazine. He published with the magazine regularly over the next few years. 1929 was a breakout year for Howard, in that the 23-year-old writer began to sell to other magazines, such as *Ghost Stories* and *Argosy*, both of whom had previously sent him hundreds of rejection slips. In 1930, he began a correspondence with weird fiction master H. P. Lovecraft which ran up to his death six years later, and is regarded as one of the great correspondence cycles in all of fantasy literature.

It was partly due to Lovecraft's encouragement that Howard created his most famous character, Conan the Cimmerian. Conan – a barbarian-turned-King during the Hyborian Age, a mythical period of some 12,000 years ago – featured in seventeen *Weird Tales* stories between 1933 and 1936, and is now regarded as having spawned the 'sword and sorcery' genre, making Howard's influence on fantasy literature comparable to that of J. R. R. Tolkien's. The Conan stories have since been adapted many times, most famously in the series of films starring Arnold Schwarzenegger.

Howard was enjoying an all-time high in sales by the beginning of 1936, but he was also deeply upset by the ill health of his mother, who had fallen into a coma. On the morning of June 11, 1936, he asked an attending nurse whether she would ever recover, and the nurse replied negatively. Howard walked to his car, parked outside the family home in Cross Plains, and shot himself. He died eight hours later, aged just thirty.

PROLOGUE

THE Slow rise and headlong fall of Rome shook the Western world. In the mushroom growth of the East, the downfall of imperial cities caused only a momentary ripple in the, swarming tides of restless humanity, and their very memory faded from the minds of men even as the crawling jungle, the drifting desert, effaced the crumbling walls and shattered towers.

Such a kingdom, Nagdragore, whose eagle-crested rajahs levied tribute from the Deccan when yellow-haired barbarians were stalking red-handed through the gates of Rome.

The glories of Nagdragore have been forgotten for a thousand years. Not even in the misty gulf of the Hindu legend where an hundred lost dynasties sleep unheeded, does any hint of that vanished realm linger. Nagdragore is one with a thousand nameless ruins; a crumbling mass of shattered stone and broken marble, lost in the waving green deeps of the blind crawling jungle.

This tale is of the times of Nagdragore's lost splendor, before she decayed and fell before the ravages of White Hun, Tatar and Mogul; a tale of the Age that saw her gleam like a scintillant jewel on the dusky breast of India, when her imperial towers rose golden, white and purple in the blue, gazing with the pride of assured destiny across the green-girdling, white-foaming Gulf of Cambay.

* * * *

"The mists are clearing."

Hairy, calloused hands rested on long ash oars and frosty eyes peered through the thinning veil. The ship was a strange one for Eastern waters; it was long, lean, low in the waist, high of stern and bows, the prow curving up into a carved dragon's head. The open build, the shield-rail, the prow marked her as a raider as clearly as did her crew: huge, flaxen-bearded warriors with cold, light eyes.

On the poop stood a small group of men, and one of these, a brooding-eyed, lowering-browed giant, cursed in his beard.

"The hordes of Halheim know where we be, or in which direction be land; yet water and food grow scant-Hrothgar, you say you sense land to the eastward, but by Thor-"

A sudden shout went up from the crew, as the rowers set their oars aback and stared with dropped jaws. Before them the fog was thinning swiftly and now hanging in the dim sky a sudden blaze of gems and marble burst upon their eyes. They glimpsed, awedly, the turrets and spires and battlements of a mighty city in the sky.

"By the blood of Loki!" swore the Viking chief, "It's Mdigaard!"

Another on the poop laughed. The Viking turned to him irritably. This man was unlike his companions; he alone bore no weapons and wore no mail, yet the rest eyed him with a sort of sullen respect. There was in his bearing a natural, lion-like dignity, a nobility of manner and a realization of power without arrogance. He was tall, as broad-shouldered and powerful as any man there, and there was about him a certain cat-like litheness that most of the massive-limbed warriors lacked. His hair was golden as theirs, his eyes as blue, but no one would have mistaken him for one of them. His strong face, browned by the sun, was quick and mobile with the whimsical half-mockery of the Celt.

"Donn Othna," said the pirate chieftain angrily, "What is your jest now?"

The other shook his head. "I only laughed to think that in yon blaze of beauty a Saxon could see the city of his cold, savage gods who build with swords and skulls rather than marble and gold."

The breeze lifted the mists and the city shone more clearly. Port, harbor and walls grew out of the fading grey with astonishing swiftness.

"Like a city of a dream," muttered Hrothgar, his cold eyes strange with wonder. "The fog was thicker than we thought, that we should have so nearly approached such a port unknowing. Look at the craft which throng her wharves. What now, Athelred?"

The giant scowled. "They have already spied us; if we flee now we will have a score of galleys swooping after us, i think. And we must have fresh water-what think you, Donn Othna?"

The Celt shrugged his mighty shoulders.

"Who am I to think anything? I am no chief among you-but if we cannot flee-and to turn now would in sooth arouse suspicion-we must put on a bold front. I see yonder many trading crafts which have the look of far-farers and it may be that these people trade with many nations and will not fall on us at sight. Not all folk are Saxons!"

Athelred snarled churlishly and shouted at the steersman who had been resting on the long sweep, staring a-gape. The long ash oars began to churn the waves again and the galley boldly swept toward the dreaming harbor. Already other crafts were putting out to meet them. Strangely-built, richly-carved galleys manned by dark-skinned men swept upon alongside and the Saxons perforce lay to, while Athelred hailed their leaders.

The Vikings gazed in amazement at the costly-ornamented ships, and at the hawk-faced, turbaned warriors whose apparel shone in silver and silk, and whose weapons shimmered with gold chasings and sparkling gems; they gaped at the heavy steel bows, the round silver-spiked, gold-braced bucklers, the long slim spears, and curved sabers. And meanwhile the Orientals stared back in equal wonder at these white-skinned, flaxen-haired giants, with their horned helmets, scale mail shirts and flaring-edged axes.

A tall, black-bearded chief stood on the ornate deck of the nearer craft and shouted to Athelred who answered him in his own tongue. Neither could understand the other and the Saxon chief began to fume with the dangerous impatience of the barbarian. There was tension in the air. The Vikings stealthily laid down their oars and felt for their axes, and aboard the other crafts bowstrings slid into the nocks of barbed arrows. Then Donn Othna, on along chance, shouted a greeting in the

Latin tongue. A change was instantly seen in the opposing chief.

He waved his arm and answered with a single word in the same tongue, which Donn Othna took to mean a friendly reply. The Celt spoke further, but the chief repeated the single Latin word and with a wave of his arm, indicated that the strangers should precede him into the port. The carles, at a growl from their chief, again took up their oars and the dragon-ship swept into the harbor and alongside the wharf with an escort of wallowing galleys on either side.

There the Eastern chief came alongside and by gesture indicated that they were to stay aboard their own craft for a while. Athelred's beard bristled at this, but there was nothing else to do. The chief strode away with a clatter of weapons and a number of tall, bearded warriors unobstrusedly took up their position on the wharves. They appeared not to notice the strangers, but Donn Othna noted that they outnumbered the dragon-ship's crew and that they bore wicked bows.

A great concourse of people carne upon the wharves, gesticulating and shouting in wonder, gazing wide-eyed at the grim white giants who stared back equally fascinated. The archers thrust back the crowd roughly, forcing them to leave a wide space clear. Donn Othna smiled; more than his more stolid companions did he appreciate the gaudy panorama of color before him.

"Donn Othna," it was Athelred growling beside him, "on which side stand you?"

"What do you mean?"

The giant waved a huge hand toward the warriors on the wharves.

"If it comes to a pitched battle, will you fight for us or will you stab me in the back?"

The big Celt laughed cynically. "Strange words to a prisoner. What avail would be a single sword against you hosts?" Then his manner changed. "Bring me the sword your men took from me; if I am to aid you I would not seem a thrall in the eyes of these people."

Athelred growled in his beard at the abrupt command, but his eyes fell before the cold gaze of the other and he shouted a command. A huge warrior presently mounted the poop, bringing with him along heavy sword in a leather sheath, attached to a broad silver-buckled belt. Donn Othna's eyes sparkled as he took the weapon and fastened it about his waist. He laid hand on the jeweled ivory hilt with its heavy silver cross-guard and drew it half from the scabbard. The double-edged blade, of a sinister blue, hummed faintly.

"By Thor!" muttered Hrothgar. "Your sword sings, Donn Othna!"

"It sings for its homecoming, Hrothgar," answered the Celt. "Now I know that yon shore is the land of Hind, for it was here that my sword was born from furnace and forge and wizard's hammer, dim ages ago. It was once a great saber belonging to a mighty Eastern emperor, whom Alexander conquered. And Alexander took it with him into Egypt where it abode until the Romans came and a consul took it for his own. Not liking the curved shape, he had a sword-maker of Damascus reshape the blade-for the Romans used straight thrusting swords. It came into Britain with Caesar and was lost to the Gaels in a great battle in the west. I myself took it from Eochaidh Mac Ailbe, king of Erin, whom I slew in a sea-fight off the western coast."

"A sword for a prince," said Hrothgar in open admiration. "Look-one comes!"

With a great shouting and clanking of arms, a mighty concourse swept down to the wharves. A thousand warriors in shining armor, on Arab barbs, camels and grunting elephants escorted one who sat in a throne-like chair high on the back of a great elephant. Donn Othna saw a lean, haughty face, black-bearded and hawk-nosed; deep dark eyes, liquid and yet keen surveyed the westerners. The Celt realized that this king, lord or whoever he was, was not of the same race as his subjects.

The cavalcade halted before the dragon-ship, trumpets split the skies in a ripping fanfare, cymbals clashed deafeningly and then a gaudily dressed chieftain spurred forward, salaamed deeply from his saddle and burst into a grandiloquent flight of words which meant exactly nothing to the gaping Occidentals. The personage on the throne-chair checked his vassal with a languid wave of a white, jewel-decked hand and spoke in clear, liquid Latin:

"He is saying, my friends, that the exalted son of the gods, the great rajah Constantius, does you the stupendous, unheard of and entirely astounding honor of coming to greet you in person."

All eyes turned toward Donn Othna, the only man aboard the long-serpent who could understand the words. The huge Saxons eyed him eagerly like great, puzzled children and it was on him that the eyes of the Orientals focussed. The tall Celt stood, arms folded, head thrown back, meeting the gaze of the rajah squarely, and for all the splendor and trappings of the Oriental, his kingship was no less apparent than the royalty of the westerner. There two natural born leaders of men faced each other, recognizing each other's regal birthright.

"I am Donn Orthna, a prince of Britain," said the Celt. "This chief is Athelred of the Saxons. We have sailed for many a weary moon and desire only peace and a chance to trade for food and water. What city is this?"

"This is Nagdragore, one of the chief principalities of India," answered the rajah. "Come ashore; ye are my guests. It's many a day since I turned my face eastward and I am hungry to speak with one in the old tongue of Rome and hear the news of the west."

"What says he? Is it peace or war? Where be we?" the questions rained on the Briton.

"We are indeed in the land of Hind," answered Donn Othna. "But yonder king is not Indian. If he be a Greek, then I am a Saxon! He bids us be his guests ashore; that may well mean prisoners, but we have no choice. Mayhap he means to deal fairly with us."

ONE

DONN OTHNA lifted a cup carved of a single jewel and drank deeply. He set it down and gazed across the richly carved teakwood table at the rajah who lounged sensuously on the silken divan. They were alone in the room except for the huge black mute who, naked except for a silk loincloth, stood just behind Constantius, holding a wide-bladed scimitar nearly as long as himself.

"Well, prince," said the rajah, toying idly with a great sapphire on his finger, "have I not played squarely with you and your men? Even now they gorge and guzzle on such meat and drink as they never dreamed existed, and rest themselves on silken couches, while musicians play stringed music for their pleasure and girls lithe as panthers dance for them. I have not even taken their axes from them-as for you, here you feast with me alone-yet I see suspicion in your eyes."

Donn Othna indicated the sword which he had unbuckled and laid on a polished bench.

"I had not unslung Alexander's sword did I not trust you. As for the Saxons-Crom's jest! They are like bears in a palace. Had you sought to disarm them their wonder had turned to desperate rage and those same axes had drunk deep in the red tides. It is not suspicion you see in my eyes but wonder. By the gods! When I was a shock-headed boy on the western marches I wondered at Tara in Erin, and gaped at Caer Odun. Then when I was a youth and raided into Roman territory, I thought Corinium, Aquae Sulis, Ebbracum and Lundinium were the mightiest cities of all the earth. When I came into manhood the memory of those was paled by my first sight of Rome, though it was crumbling under the defiling feet of Goth and Vandal. And Rome seems but a village when I gaze at the crowned spires and golden-chased towers of Nagdragore!"

Constantius nodded, a tinge of bitterness in his eyes. "It is an empire worth fighting for, and once I had dreams of spanning the land of India from sea to sea-but tell me of Rome and Byzantium; it has been a long time since I turned my face eastward. Then the German barbarians were overrunning the Roman borders, Genseric was pillaging the imperial city herself and rumors of a strange and terrible people came even to Byzantium which writhed under the heel of the Ostrogoth."

"The Huns!" exclaimed Donn Othna, his face lighting fiercely. "Aye, they came out of the East like a wind of death like a swarm of locusts. They drove the Goths, the Franks and the Vandals before them and the Teutons trampled Rome in their flight. Then with the sea before them, they could fly no further. They turned at bay, the two hosts met at Chalons-by the gods, there was a sword-quenching! There the ravens fed and the axes were glutted redly! They rolled on us like a black wave, and as a wave breaks on the rocks, they broke on the German shield wall and the ranks of Aetius' legions."

"You were there?" exclaimed Constantius.

"Aye! With five hundred of my tribesmen!" Donn Othna's fierce eyes blazed and he smote his fist resoundingly upon the table. "We sailed with those British legions who went to the succor of Rome-and came no more to their native soil. On the plains of Gaul and Italy their bones rot-and those of many a western clansman who never bowed to Rome, but who followed his civilized kin to the wars.

"All day we fought and at the end, the Huns broke; by Crom, my sword was red and clotted from pommel to point, and i could scarcely lift my arm. Of my five hundred warriors, fifty lived!

"Well, Votigern had called in the Jutes to aid him against the Picts and the Angles, and Saxons followed them like hungry wolves. I returned to Britain and in the whirlwind of war that swept the southern coasts, I fell captive to this Athelred, who knowing my name and rank, wished to hold me for ransom. But a strange thing came to pass-"

Donn Othna paused and laughed shortly.

"We of the west hate long and well, and our Gaelic cousins make a cult of revenge, but by Crom, I never knew what the lust for vengeance could be until we sighted the ships of Asgrimm the Angle. This sea-king has an old feud with Athelred and he gave chase with his ten long-serpents.

14

By Crom, he chased us half around the world! He hung to our stern like a hunting dog and we could not elude him.

"We raced him around the coast of Gaul and down past Spain, and when we would have turned into the Mediterranean he crowded us close and drove us past the Gates of Hercules. South and forever south we fled, past sullen, steaming coasts, dank with swamp or dark with jungle, where black people wild and naked shouted and shot arrows at us.

"At last we rounded a cape and headed east, and somewhere there we shook off our pursuers. Since then we have sailed and rowed at random. So you see, King Constantius, my news is nearly a year old."

The rajah's deep dark eyes were pensive with inner thought. He sighed and drank deep of the goblet the black slave filled and tasted first.

"Nearly twenty years ago I sailed from Byzantium with Cyprian traders bound for Alexandria. I was but a youth, ignorant and full of wonder at the world, but with royal blood in my veins. From Alexandria I wandered by devious ways to Damascus and there I joined a caravan returning to Shiraz in Persia. Later I sought pearls on the Gulf of Oman and it was there that I was taken captive by a Maldive pirate who sold me on the slave block at Nagdragore. I need not repeat to you the devious route by which I reached the throne.

"The old dynasty was crumbling, ready to fall; Nagdragore was harried by incessant wars with neighboring kingdoms. It was a red trail, black with plot and treachery that I followed, but today I am rajah of Nagdragore-though the throne rocks beneath my feet."

Constantius rested his elbows on the table and his chin in his hands; his great brooding eyes fixed themselves on the blond giant opposite him.

"You are a prince likewise, though your palace be a wattle hut," he said. "We be of the same world, though I had my birth at one end, and you at the other end of that world. I need men I can trust. My kingdom is divided against itself and I play one chief against the other to the hurt of Nagdragore, but to mine own gain. My chief foes are Anand Mulhar and Nimbaydur Singh. The one is rich, cowardly and avaricious; too cautious and too suspicious to oppose me openly. The other is young, passionate, romantic and brave, but a victim of moneylenders who watch the way the fish leaps.

"The common people hate me because they love Nimbaydur Singh who has a trace of royal blood in his veins. The nobles-the Rajputs-dislike me because I am an outlander. But I rule the moneylenders, and through them, Nagdragore.

"The war is a more or less secret one in which I am ground between Anand Mulhar on the one side and

Nimbaydur Singh on the other, yet still hold in my hands the reins of power. They hate each other too much to combine against me.

"But it is the silent assassin's dagger I have to fear. I half trust my guard, but half trust is little better than full suspicion and far more dangerous. That is why I came down to the wharves to greet you myself. Will you and these barbarians remain here in the palace and do battle for me if the occasion arise?

"I could not make you officially my bodyguard. It would offend the nobles and all would rise instantly. But I will ostensibly make you part of the army; you will remain here in the palace and you, prince, shall be my cup companion."

Donn Othna grinned a slow, lazy grin, and reached for the wine pitcher.

"I will talk to Athelred," said he. "I think he will agree."

TWO

THE BRITON found Athelred sitting cross-legged on a silken couch, tearing at a huge quarter of roast lamb, between enormous gulps of Indian wine. The Saxon growled a greeting and continued to gorge and guzzle, while Donn Othna seated himself and glanced quizzically about him. The pirate crew sprawled at ease among the cushions on the marble floor or wandered about the great room, gazing curiously up at the jeweled dome high overhead or staring out the golden-barred windows into courts with flowering trees and exotic blossoms scenting the air, or into colonnaded chambers where fountains flung a silvery sheen high into the air. They were curious and delighted as children and suspicious as wolves. Each kept his curved-handled, wicked-headed axe close to his hand.

"What now, Donn Othna?" mumbled Athelred, munching away without a pause.

"What would you?" parried the Briton.

"Why," the pirate waved a half-gnawed bone about him, "here's loot that would make Hengist's eyes open and Cerdic's mouth water. Let us do this: in the night we will rise stealthily and set fire to the palace; then in the confusion we will snatch such plunder as we can easily bear away and hack our way to our ship which lies unguarded along the docks.

Then, ho, for the western seas! When my people see what we bring, there will be a hundred dragon-ships following us! We will plunder Nagdragore as Genseric plundered Rome and carve us out a kingdom with our axes."

"Would it draw your sea-wolves from Britain," said Donn Othna grimly, "I might agree. But it's a plan too mad for even a Saxon to try. Even if I could overlook the treachery to our host, we could never cover half the distance to the ship. A hundred and fifty men cut their way through fifty thousand? Think no more of it."

"What then?" growled Athelred. "By Thor, it seems our positions have changed! Aboard ship you were our prisoner. Now it seems we are yours! We are hereditary foes; how do I know you mean to deal squarely with us? How do I know what you and the king have been jabbering to each other? Maybe you plan to cut our throats."

"And not knowing you must take my word for it," answered the prince calmly. "I have no love for you or your race, though I know you as brave men. But here it is to our advantage to act in concert. Without me you have no interpreter; without you I have no armed force to strengthen my claim to respect. Constantius has offered us service in his palace guards. I trust him no more than you trust me; he will deal us false the moment it is to his advantage. But until such time it is to our advantage to comply with his request. If I know men, niggardliness is not one of his faults. We will live

19

well on his bounty. Just now he needs our swords. Later that need may pass and we may take ship again-but understand, Athelred, this service I do you now is my ransom. I am no longer your prisoner and if I go aboard your ship again, I am a free man, whom you will set on British soil without price."

"I swear it by my sword," grunted Athelred, and Donn Othna nodded, satisfied, knowing the blunt Saxon was a man of his word.

"The East is fraught with unlimited possibilities," said the Briton. "Here a bold heart and a keen sword can accomplish as much as they can in the West and the reward is greater, if more fleeting. Just now, I doubt if Constantius trusts me fully. I must prove that we can be of value to him."

The chance came sooner than he had hoped. In the days following, Donn Othna and his comrades abode in the mazes of the Eastern city, wondering at the strange contrasts: the splendor and riches of the nobles, the poverty and squalor of the poor. Nor was the least paradox he who sat upon the throne.

Donn Othna sat in the golden-leaf chamber and drank wine with the rajah Constantius, while the great silent black man served them. The British prince gazed in wonder at the rajah. Constantius drank deeply and unwisely. He was drunk, his strange eyes darker and more liquid than ever.

"You are a relief as well as a protection to me, Donn Othna," said he, with a slight hiccup. "I can be my true self with you-at least I assume it to be my true self. I trust you because you bring the clean, straightforward power of the western winds and the clean salt tang of the western seas with you. I need not be forever on my guard. I tell you, Donn Othna, this business of empire is not one that makes for ease or happiness. Had I to live my life over again, I would rather be what once I was: a clean-limbed, brown-skinned youth, diving for pearls in the Oman Gulf and flinging them away to dark-eyed Arab girls.

"But the purple is my curse and my birthright, just as it's yours. I am rajah not because I was wise or foolish but because I have the blood of emperors in my veins and I followed a destiny I could not avoid. You, too, will live to press a throne and curse the crown that wearies your tired neck. Drink!"

Donn Othna waved away the proffered goblet.

"I have drunk enough and you far too much," he said bluntly. "By Crom, I have found to be much of a hashish eater and more of a drunkard. You are incredibly wise and incredibly foolish. How can a man like you be a king?"

Constantius laughed. "A question that had cost another man his head. I will tell you why I am king: because I can flatter men and see through their flattery; because I know the weaknesses of strong men; because I know how to use money; because I have no scruples whatever, and resort to any method, fair or foul, to gain my ends. Because, being born to the West and raised in the East, the guile of both worlds is in me. Because, though I am in the main a fool, I have flashes of real genius, beyond the power of a consistently wise man. And because-and all my other gifts were useless without it--I have the power of molding women as wax in my hands. Let me look in any woman's eyes and hold her close to me, and she is my slave forever."

Donn Othna shrugged his mighty shoulders and set down his goblet.

"The East draws me with a strange fascination," said he, "though I had rather rule a tribe of shock-headed Cymry. But, by Crom, your ways are devious and strange."

Constantius laughed and rose unsteadily. The retiring of the rajah was attended to only by the great black mute. Don n Othna slept in a chamber adjoining the golden-leaf room.

And now Donn Othna, dismissing his own slave, stepped to the heavily barred window that looked out on an inner court, and breathed deep the spice scents of the Orient. The dreaming antiquity of India touched his eyelids with slumberous fingers and in the deeps of his soul dim racial memories stirred. After all, he felt a certain kinship with these hawk-faced, keen-eyed Rajputs. They were of his blood, if the ancient legends were true that told of the days when the sons of Aryan were one great tribe in the mist-dim ages before Nimbaydur Singh's ancestors broke from the nation in that great southern drift, and before Donn Othna's ancestors took up the long trek westward.

A faint sound brought him back to the present. A quick stride took him across the room where he gazed into the golden-leaf chamber through a cloth-of-gold curtain. A dancing girl had entered the chamber and Donn Othna wondered how she had gotten past the swordsmen stationed outside the door. She was a slim young thing, lithe and beautiful, her scanty silken girdle and golden breastplates accentuating her sinuous loveliness. She approached the huge black who stared at her in sullen wonder and menace. She approached him, her red lips pleading, her deep eyes luring, her little hands outstretched and upturned beseechingly. Donn Othna could not understand her low tones-though he had learned much of the Rajput language-but he saw the black shake his bullet head and lift his huge scimitar threateningly.

She was close to the mute now-and she moved like a striking cobra. From somewhere about her scanty garments she flashed a dagger and with the same motion she flicked it under the mute's heart. He swayed like a great black idol, the sword fell from his nerveless hands and he fell across it, his face writhing in the agony of effort as his withered tongue sought to sound a warning to his master. Then blood burst from that silently gaping mouth and the great slave lay still.

The girl sprang quickly and silently toward the door, but Donn Othna was ahead of her in a single bound. She checked herself for a fleeting second, then sprang at his throat like a fury. The dances of the East make their devotees lithe and steel-like in every thew. Ages later when westerners again invaded the East, they found that a slim nautch girl could prove more than a match for a man. But those men had never tugged at a galley oar, wielded a twenty pound battle-axe or reined four wild chariot horses back on their haunches. Donn Othna caught the feline fury that was thrusting so earnestly for his life, disarmed her with little effort and tucked her under his arm like a child.

He was rather uncertain as to his next step when out of the royal bedchamber came the rajah, his eyes still clouded somewhat with wine. A single glance showed him what had occurred.

"Another woman assassin?" he asked casually. "My throne against your sword, Donn Othna, Anand Mulhar sent her. Nimbaydur Singh is too upright for such tricks-the poor fool." He casually touched the body of his faithful slave with his toe, but made no comment.

"What shall I do with the spit-fire?" asked Donn Othna. "She's too young to hang and if you let her go-"

Constantius shook his head. "Neither one nor the other; let me have her."

Donn Othna handed her to the rajah as if she were an infant, glad to be rid of the scratching, biting little devil.

But at the first touch of Constantius' hands she fell quiet, trembling like a high-strung steed. The rajah sat down on a divan and forced the girl to her knees before him, without harshness and without mercy. She whimpered a little, far more afraid of the Greek's calmness than she had been of Donn Othna's anger. One white jeweled hand held her slim wrist, the other rested on her head forcing her to look up into the rajah's face with eyes that sought desperately to escape his steady stare.

"You are very young and very foolish," said Constantius in a deliberate tone. "You came here to murder me because some evil master sent you-" his hand slowly caressed her as a man pets a dog. "Look into my eyes; I am your rightful master. I will not harm you; you will remain with me and you will love me."

"Yes, master," the girl answered in a small voice like a girl in a trance; her eyes did not try to evade Constantius now. They were very wide and filled with a strange new light; she leaned to the rajah's caress. He smiled and the quality of that smile made him strangely handsome.

"Tell me who you are and who sent you," he commanded, and to Donn Othna's utter amazement, the girl bowed her head obediently.

"I am Yatala; my master Anand Mulhar sent me to kill you, master. For more than a moon now, I have danced in the palace. For my master put me on the block and so contrived that your wizard bought me among other dancing girls. It was well planned, master. I came tonight and made eyes at the guards without; then when they let me approach, seeing that I was little and unarmed, I blew a secret dust into their eyes, so that deep sleep came upon them. Then taking a dagger from one, I entered-and you know the rest, master."

She hid her face on Constantius' knees and the rajah looked up at Donn Othna with a lazy smile.

"What think you of my power over women now, Donn Othna?"

"You are a devil," answered the prince frankly. "I would have taken oath no torture could have wrung from that girl what she has just told you freely-hark!"

A stealthy footstep sounded without. The girl's eyes flared with sudden terror.

"Beware, my lord!" she cried. "That is Tamur, Anand Mulhar's strangler; he followed me to make sure-"

Donn Othna whirled toward the door-it opened to reveal a terrible shape. Tamur was taller and heavier than the powerful Briton. Naked except for a loincloth, his dusky bronze skin rippled over knots and coils of iron muscle's. His limbs were like oak and iron, yet lithe and springy as a tiger's, his shoulders incredibly wide. A short tree-like neck held a bestial head. The low, slanting forehead, the flaring nostrils, the cruel gash of a mouth, the close-ears, the ape-like shaven skull, all betrayed the human beast, the born blood-letter. In his girdle was twisted the implement of his trade: a sinister silken cord. In his right hand he bore a curved saber.

Donn Othna took in this formidable figure in one glance, then' he was springing to the attack with the headlong savagery of his race. His sword flashed through the air in a blazing blue arc just as the other struck. Here was no hesitant caution on either side. Both sprang and struck simultaneously, quick to fling all on a single blow. And in mid-air the curved blade and the straight blade met with a resounding clash. The scimitar shivered to a thousand ringing sparks and, before the Briton could strike again, the strangler dropped his hilt and like a striking snake caught his white-skinned foe in a fierce grip.

The British prince let go his sword, useless at such close-quarters, and returned the grapple. In an instant he knew that he was pitted against a skilled and cruel wrestler. The smooth, naked body of the Indian was like a great snake and as hard to hold. But not for naught had Donn Othna held his own with trained Roman wrestlers of old. Now he blocked and fended shrewd thrust of knee and elbow and the clutch of iron fingers that sought cruel, maiming holds, while he launched an attack of his own. The thin veneer of civilization, acquired from contact with his Romanized neighbors, had vanished in the heat of battle, and it was a white-skinned barbarian, wild as any Goth or Saxon, who tore and snarled in the golden-leaf room of Nagdragore's rajahs.

Donn Othna saw, over Tamur's heaving shoulder, Constantius approaching with the sword he had dropped and, blue eyes blazing with battle-lust, he snarled for the rajah to keep back and let him finish his own fight.

Chest to chest, the giants strove, reeling back and forth, close-clinched, but still upright, each foiling every effort of the other. Tamur's thumb gouged at Donn Othna's eye, but the prince sank his head against the other's massive chest, shifted his hold, and the strangler was forced to cease gouging and break the Briton's hold, to save his own spine.

Again Tamur caught Donn Othna's arm in a sudden bone-breaking crossbar grip that had snapped the elbow like a twig had not the British prince suddenly driven his head hard and desperately into the Indian's face. Blood spattered as Tamur's head snapped back and Donn Othna, following his advantage, back-heeled him and threw him. Both crashed heavily on the floor, but the strangler writhed from under the Briton, and the latter found his neck menaced by a grip that bent his head back at a sickening angle.

With a gasp he tore free, just as Tamur drove his knee agonizingly into the Briton's groin. Then as the white man's iron grip involuntarily relaxed, the brown man leaped free, whipping the deadly cord from his girdle. Donn Othna rose more slowly, nauseated with the pain of that foul thrust; and Tamur, with an inhuman croak of triumph, sprang and cast his cord. The Briton heard the girl scream, as he felt the thin length whip like a serpent about his throat, instantly cutting off his breath. But at the same instant he struck out blindly and terrifically, his clenched iron fist meeting Tamur's jaw like a mallet meeting a ship's side. The strangler dropped like a log and Donn Othna, gasping, tore the cord from his tortured throat and flung it aside, just as Tamur scrambled to his feet, eyes glaring like a madman's.

The Briton fell on him raging, battering him with sledge-hammer blows, gained from long hours of practice with cestus. Such an attack was beyond Tamur's skill to cope with; the East has not the instinct of striking with the clenched fist. A swing that smashed full in his mouth splattered blood and splintered teeth and he retaliated with the only sort of blow he knew-an open-handed, full-armed slap to the side of the head that staggered Donn Othna and filled his eyes with momentary spark-short darkness. But instantly he returned the blow with a smash that sank deep in Tamur's midriff and dropped him to his knees, gasping and writhing.

The strangler grappled Donn Othna's legs and dragged him down, and once more they battled and tore close-clinched. But the ravening Briton felt his foe grow weaker and, redoubling the fury of his attack, like a tiger maddened by the blood scent, he bore the Indian backward and down, sought and found a deadly hold at last and strangled the strangler, sinking his iron fingers deeper and deeper until he felt the life flow out from under them and the writhing body stiffened.

Then Donn Othna rose and shook the blood and sweat from his eyes and smiled grimly at the spellbound rajah who stood like one frozen, still dangling Alexander's sword.

"Well, Constantius," said Donn Othna, "you see I am worthy of your trust."

www.ingramcontent.com/pod-product-compliance
Lightning Source LLC
Chambersburg PA
CBHW030136260626
47156CB00008B/2968